The Devil's Newspaper

AND OTHER STORIES

Nan Becklean

1st Edition

Copyright © 2012 Nan Becklean

A CIP catalogue record for this book is available from the US Library of Congress.

ISBN: 978-0-9884868-3-6

CONTENTS

In memory of Austin Tobin, husband, partner and lover of short stories

ALLISON

We met ten years ago on a fundraising committee for the school and have been friends ever since. Her husband, Martin, and my husband, Phil, got along pretty well so we often did things together on weekends – went to the movies, played bridge, had each other for dinner – like that. But it was our unhappy marriages that drew us together, kept us on the phone for hours every week while the kids were in school and our husbands, at work. For a few months we'd been covering for each other when we met our lovers.

Last Thursday we went into the city late in the afternoon. We told Martin and Phil we were spending the night at my sister's apartment – only half true – I was; Allison wasn't. And we said we were going to see a foreign movie together, again not quite true. I saw *Crouching Tiger, Hidden Dragon* with my lover, and Allison saw *Amelie* with hers. She didn't tell me what his name was although I told her mine; hers was someone from our community whereas mine was not and there was little chance of her ever meeting him. *Amelie* was scheduled for seven and since I didn't have to meet my guy for half an hour, I hid across the street from that movie theater behind a sign in front of a bistro and watched.

I was pretty surprised when I saw Bill DeVera, husband of our church deaconess, walk into the theater. I could see Allison's white blouse in the darkness beside him when he bought the tickets. He wasn't the type to have an affair – such a straight arrow, and I thought, boring. Bill didn't see me – but then he wasn't looking for trouble way downtown in the Village.

The next morning Allison and I met for a late breakfast near Grand Central to go over our alibi. It hardly mattered which movie we elected to have seen together since neither of our husbands would ever be interested enough to ask the titles or the plots. Both hated watching movies with subtitles so they'd never go themselves. On the other hand, someone else might ask so we settled on *Crouching Tiger, Hidden Dragon* and went over the details of the movie together. We decided to say we'd gone for a late dinner afterwards at a popular Italian restaurant near my sister's apartment and ordered scampi. There weren't any other loose ends.

Allison grabbed the Post – I had a paperback in my purse – and we caught the 11:05 for Marsbury. I caught a glimpse of the paper's headline – MAN CRUSHED UNDER SUBWAY.

It was seamless. I called Phil from home and thanked him for cleaning up the kitchen and getting the children to school on time. Later, a neighbor called, said she was at the DeVera's and that Gail's husband, Bill, had been identified as the man killed on the tracks. Speechless, I sank into a chair.

Finally I said, "Good God, what a terrible thing. How did it happen?"

"The police think he was pushed. They're investigating," she said.

"Horrible," I said, hearing my heart in my ear. "How's Gail?"

"Sedated and asleep upstairs. She was hysterical. To make it worse, she found out she was pregnant on Monday. Bill was so happy. She said he told her this would be his last overnight in town even if it meant changing jobs. Sad."

After a long pause I said, "I'll bring something over for Gail as soon as I can stand up and think straight. A casserole maybe?"

"That would be lovely. Allison, bless her heart, just came by with a chocolate cake."

Another long pause. What could I say?

"How nice of her," I whispered at long last. Now and forever – my lips are sealed.

CAUSA MORTIS

Dear Jessica,

Don't freak out. You're not expecting this so please fold this letter up now, go home, fix a cup of tea and sit down before you read any further. I mean it.

....

....

All the above space is to make it plain that I'm serious. Go home. Fix tea. Sit down. Are you set? Not quite? Here's some more space.

....

....

Okay. I'm sorry, sweetheart, but what follows is not pleasant though I've tried to be light-hearted. I've written down what's been happening – see below – and am going to put this in my safety deposit box for you to read after my death – that's why I had you take a key after co-signing for it at the bank last week. By the way, please don't forget death is not the absolute end – we'll see each other later – *much* later because I'm sure you'll live to be a hundred years old at least. This is FYI just in case I happen to die in an accident of some kind and the circumstances seem similar to what I tell you about in this letter. At least you'll know it wasn't an accident but that I was, in fact, murdered and you and Matt can then decide what to do about it – if anything.

First of all who would do such a thing? Your stepfather for example was certainly a suspect – yes, that sweet empathetic soul. I couldn't help but wonder because he was always here when worrisome things happened and so I had to consider the logic of it, however disagreeable. But the good news is – he's not any more. Next question: Why would anyone would want to kill me? There are two easy answers: my stock portfolio and the compound. In the natural order of things, Jack – being male and seven years older than I – would die first in which case his daughter wouldn't inherit anything of mine – and in fact I'd inherit one-third of everything of his.

By the way, I can't transfer my portfolio to you and Matt because Jack and I need the interest and dividends to supplement Jack's pension. Now about the compound – it's been in our family forever but, apparently, Jack's daughter would like it to be in hers as well. She's said so in a joking way through the years, but, as you know, people have a way of saying, "just kidding" after they've made a remark they really mean. If I were dead – as I must be or you wouldn't be reading this – one-third of everything I own belongs to your stepfather and when he dies he will, of course, leave whatever he inherits from me to his daughter.

I can't blame her for wanting to own a part of the big lake house and the six cottages. It is, after all, a spectacular place – but arranging for my premature demise seems to be going a bit far. I know you and your brother – I assume he'll fly over from Paris for my memorial service – would invite Doris and her family to come up for weekends or even longer if the place were yours outright. However, now that she's probably engineered my death – I'd rather you didn't.

Now this is important: You can bypass the will by executing the quit-claim I signed a while back in your and Matt's favor – it's also in the safety deposit box –

and thus should be able to hold on to the compound *in toto*. After all, my murder is not going to be easy to prove and I'm not suggesting you should even bother to try. Perhaps you can use this letter as evidence but if not I just hope it points you in the right direction so you find a way of proving what happened assuming, that is, you have the energy for it. I realize how expensive and exhausting going to court would be so it may not be worth it to you and Matt. Still I want you to know the facts just in case you want to proceed.

Okay – here we go:

This past July I nearly fell down the basement stairs. If I'd been carrying anything in my arms, as I usually am, I probably would have broken my neck – but I was able to grab hold of the banister with my right hand – I was holding a bag of oranges to put in the downstairs refrigerator with the left – and so all that happened was I fell to my knees sideways and banged one of them up pretty badly. Not an unusual occurrence you might say but I noticed afterwards there was something greasy on my right shoe and, when I checked the top step, sure enough, it was slick as New York Ned. Didn't think too much about it at the time, though, when I thought back on it later, I remembered that Doris had stopped by that morning for coffee on her way home from errands and had the time and privacy to do anything she pleased. I was weeding outside the whole time she was here – she poured herself a cup – came outside for a short chat, then went into the office to see her father. I know it's circumstantial but someone definitely oiled the step – it smelled like Crisco – and the only other person who could have done so was Jack. Of course Jack could also have been the one to take the fall but, as everyone including his daughter knows, he has a trick knee and almost never goes down those stairs to the basement or, for that matter, upstairs to the second floor.

Come August the same thing happened. You can be sure I was more careful after the near fall the month before and never went down without holding the banister before I put a foot on the stair, but, this time much more of the step was oiled and the next one as well. It wasn't Crisco this time – possibly olive oil – maddening to think that Doris used my treasured extra-virgin cold-pressed. On the other hand, maybe she brought her own. You're probably wondering why I left her alone in the house and the answer is I didn't. I was out when she came to see her father and he forgot to mention her visit when I came back from having my hair done; he told me about it later. Doris knows I have a standing appointment at 9:30 on Fridays.

By the way, I didn't say a word to anyone about the July incident – Jack or my friends would have thought I was paranoid or at the very least, exaggerating, as I must admit I'm guilty of doing from time to time to make stories a little more interesting. As for you – you were changing jobs and thinking of getting a divorce at the time so I wasn't going to bother you with my suspicions. Your brother, as you probably know, thinks I'm batty so I could hardly mention it to him during one of our infrequent and brief phone conversations.

I don't know how many more times this happened but I got in the habit of carefully placing folded newspaper on the steps before I went down to the basement. I still held on to the banister but never slipped again or hurt myself. Yes, I looked to see if there was some hidden leak that could have made the steps slippery – even had our handyman check it out when he was doing some other repairs but nada. Also, I always removed the newspaper on my way back up. Occasionally, there was oil on the bottom side. Since it only happened when Doris had been around I came to the happy conclusion it wasn't my dear husband.

At the same time I started to have problems with the car. You might say *no surprise – that old thing –* and you'd be right. We should have gotten rid of it long ago, bought a new one. Well now your stepfather will have to do exactly that because both the thirteen-year-old Taurus and your nearly sixty-five year old mother are probably history. I hope our final gasps were down in the gully off Breakneck Hill or some such and not on the Post Road where I might have plowed into a bunch of cars and killed a dozen people including children. At first I thought it was just the car in extremis when a wheel nearly came off and I had to have the car towed to Marsbury Auto. Gene, the owner, scratched his head said it was odd because we had purchased four new wheels from him the previous spring and he had put them on himself so he was none too pleased the lugnuts were loose though he was certain it wasn't his fault. I thought no more about it until the same thing happened again – different wheel. Of course Gene had checked all the wheels after the first mishap and said they were fine. After the second occurrence, he said I should report it to the police and I did just that but they didn't seem to think it was worth investigating. *Note: once you're a senior citizen many people take what you have to say with a big grain of salt.* Oh, by the way, I forgot to mention that both times the wheels were compromised it was after I had been out in the pickup buying plants and mulch for the new perennial beds and both times Jack said Doris had been over for a visit. She stops by a lot and most of the time I'm home. In any case, if she wanted to do anything to my car no one would notice unless they were standing right next to her because, as you may remember, our enormous pine trees hide the driveway from both the house and the road. Also, these days both cars are always parked outside because the entire garage is filled with gardening equipment.

After the second wheel came loose I decided I'd better discuss the situation with Jack but then I couldn't get myself to bring it up. He wouldn't have believed Doris could do such things so what was the point? Last week I decided to take matters into my own hands and started driving Jack's pickup whenever possible. I'd throw a bunch of stuff in the back to take to the dump so he wouldn't think it was strange – but how long can that go on? By the way Gene would be a good witness if something happens to me in the car – and I'm pretty sure the police recorded my complaint. Also, I finally told Theresa and Abby the whole story – they're such good friends and completely discrete – I'll give them each a copy of this letter when I see them later today. The point is you can call them as soon as you calm down. At least you'll have people to talk to who will be equally horrified.

I'm doing everything I can think of to stay in one piece – but who knows what other mischief Doris will get up to. If she has a lugnut removal tool – what other devices might she may be the proud owner of? My hope is you won't see or read this letter until many years hence – after I die of natural causes that is – but no question Jack's daughter seems determined to find a way to do away with me. The whole thing is even more shocking because I always liked her and thought she liked me.

There's an aphorism that says something like this: if you live long enough you'll experience everything. I guess that includes solving my own murder!

Vale sed non perpetuo. Take good care. I love you and Matt, too,

Mom

THE DEVIL'S NEWSPAPER

Peter was waiting for the phone to ring – not something he usually did. His clients, wife, even his friends were the ones kept waiting while he made a call or signed a document. But he wasn't in his office or at home; he was on vacation. He glanced at the DelRay paper and laughed. No wonder polls showed people who lived outside metropolitan areas didn't know what the president's name was – the headlines were all about sports or murders.

He turned on the TV. There was a movie he liked but had seen three times. He should have brought along a couple of paperback mysteries. They would have come in handy on the plane when Leila wasn't speaking to him.

He was glad she'd taken his suggestion and gone for a pedicure and manicure. They'd already decided not to have lunch together. He had a tennis date in half an hour, eleven-thirty, with a guy he met in the hotel bar shortly after they'd unpacked and changed into more casual clothes the night before. His name was Alex. Seemed nice enough.

The phone rang. It was Leila. "After I finish here I'm going to the beach," she said. "Just didn't want you to worry."

"Okay, thanks." When she was pleasant it made him forget how hard she was to live with.

The phone rang again. His mother. She was taking care of Emily and Derek.

"Hi dear," she said. "How is she?"

"Seems okay."

"Is she taking her meds?"

"Don't know. I'm afraid to ask. Sometimes she goes nuts when I do. How are the kids?"

"Fine. I had the sitter take them to the park so I could be alone when we talked." His mother paused. "After everything you told me last week I haven't been able to think of much else. I knew Leila was high-strung but..."

"What?"

"I didn't know she'd cut her wrists a half dozen times or burned all your pictures from before you were married or cut up your clothes. What kind of person does such things?"

"An unhappy person – a depressed person. I don't really know. The shrink doesn't say much. He's her shrink so of course he doesn't."

"Do you really think this vacation is going to help?"

"Probably not but what choice do I have? I've got to think of the children. Divorce isn't a good option. She's been a good mother."

"Except when she left them alone in the house last month. Anything could have happened."

"It's hard to know what she's capable of sometimes," he said.

"That's what worries me."

"I shouldn't have told you. There's nothing you can do and I can handle whatever happens just as I've been doing all along.

"Okay, I'll try," his mother said.

"Try what?"

"Not to worry."

"Good and, Mom, thank you for taking the kids on such short notice. Tell Dad."

"I will, dear. Goodbye."

Leila lay on her chair and squinted at the sun-bleached ocean no longer the deep blue-green of morning. Her stomach was flat despite her two tandem pregnancies – the children were eleven months apart – but there were stretch marks on either side of her navel. She would never be the same. I should have had my tubes tied after Emily, she thought. I'll make an appointment when we get home. I can't go through it again. Her mother was right, had always been right, men don't understand. They could – but don't want to. Peter was smart, made a ton of money but he looked past her when she talked and was always on his way out – to the office, tennis court, golf course, wherever. Only in sleep did he look completely relaxed and in the moment. Even when they had sex she felt he had his eye on the clock.

He said he loved her and if she knew what that meant maybe she'd believe it. From her experience love was a con. He said she was beautiful and sexy. She didn't feel it. He bought her jewelry. She didn't wear it. She wanted to be left alone for a long time with no one, child or husband, pawing at her body.

A child, sand pail and shovel in hand, appeared at her side. "Hi, I'm Jamie," he said.

"Hi," said Leila.

"I'm collecting shells. You want one?"

"Sure,"

"Here," said Jamie.

It was a beauty – luminous pink and pale green satin inside, smooth and brilliant white out.

"This is too nice," said Leila. "You keep it. Better yet give it to your mother."

"Okay, when she comes down for lunch," said Jamie. He stood there. "Um," he said.

"Yes?"

"Could I touch you?"

"Sure," said Leila.

Jamie placed a sandy forefinger on her upper arm and held it there a few seconds. He took it away and frowned. "You're not," he said.

"Not what?"

"Hot," said Jamie. "My daddy said you were."

"Just goes to show," said Leila.

"What?"

"Don't believe everything you hear."

"Okay," said Jamie.

"Or read."

"I can't read yet," said Jamie.

"Just remember what I said. It'll come in handy when the devil hands you his newspaper."

They looked into each other's eyes. The child's were gray-blue like Peter's, like the sun-bleached ocean at noon.

Jamie turned and walked to where the sand was wet and the water could just reach his toes. Beyond, when it receded, was a new supply of shells.

Leila admired her hands and toes, the matching coral of their nails, and the perfect tan of her arms and legs. Whatever it's all for I don't know, she thought. Along the inside of her wrists were the tiny white lines of her suicide attempts. Pretty half bracelets, she thought and remembered with pleasure the brightness of her blood when it started to flow.

Peter's bathing trunks were in the bottom drawer of the big dresser he and Leila shared in large room overlooking the ocean. He pulled them out. His face was a mottled red, his hair and tennis clothes soaked with sweat. A swim before lunch would be just the ticket. Then he'd dry off and meet Alex on the terrace where they could have a drink. He unstuck his clothes from his body, peeled them off, opened the bathroom door and tossed them to the side of the sink and grabbed a towel from the rack. There was a noise. He looked around the corner, pulled aside the shower curtain to find Leila in the tub, water to her neck, face still rosy from the sun, dark eyes open, blood trickling bright red from her wrists.

"My God," he said. "My God!"

"Sorry," said Leila.

"Did you take your meds?"

"I forgot."

She had waited until she heard Peter come into the bedroom. Then she propped one wrist on the edge of the tub, slit it, changed hands, and when he opened the bathroom door she slit, with difficulty, the other one. The knife dropped from her hand down the side of the tub onto the tile floor.

"Sorry," she said again and lifted her shoulders to be helped out.

"So am I," said Peter.

Then he closed the shower curtain, shut the bathroom door, put on his trunks, threw the towel over his shoulder and went for a swim in the gray-blue sea.

A GOOD WOMAN

Aunt Jane didn't want to go. "Too many people on the road who don't know how to drive. And the trucks!" she added, "I believe they'd just as soon kill you." She put down TV Guide and picked up her knitting. She was making herself a warm hat for the Chicago winter to come.

"There's supposed to be a bad storm," said eight-year-old Melissa from under the piano where she and Bingo liked to hide.

"If we leave early we'll be fine," said Steve. He had made reservations a month in advance at Bestview, a popular motel with an Olympic size pool on the way to Orlando, and he wasn't about to cancel.

"A tornado's what I heard," said Aunt Jane. "I know about those darn twisters. You don't want to mess with them."

Jeff looked up from the checkerboard. He was nearly eleven.

"It's your turn," said Maggie, his twin. "Play."

"You ever seen a tornado, Aunt Jane?"

"Lots of them."

"Wow," said Jeff. "I'd like to get up real close to one."

"Over my dead body," said Dolores, his mother. She spent nights imagining horrible things happening to her children – Jeff in particular because he was always hanging from a tree or walking on a fence. Once he fell out his bedroom window and broke an arm. She never understood how it happened.

"The weather-watchers do it."

"You make things up. There's no such thing as weather-watchers!" said Melissa who figured she was smarter than just about anyone. "I've never heard of them!"

"I have," said Aunt Jane.

Steve wanted to change the subject but there'd be no shutting her up. For one thing Steve was raised to be polite and for another he was in her debt. She had taken care of his mother, her elder sister, for nearly a year before she died. The Targetts gave up their dining room to make room for his mother's electric bed and wheelchair and a rollaway bed for Aunt Jane. Steve would never forget how labor intensive it was to feed and bathe his mother, let alone do what was necessary to keep her in clean diapers. His mother had been a thin woman but the effort to lift her was still enormous and Steve wasn't usually at home to help. Now Aunt Jane was welcome to visit whenever she liked and was always invited to go with them on vacation. He'd been hoping she'd say no to this one and take a flight back to Chicago, but however much she griped about the destination – she was still there.

"Well then – you have to tell us about them," said Steve, "but first, it seems to me that if you're not happy about driving to Disneyland tomorrow, maybe you should take the seven-thirty flight out. It'll get you into Chicago around nine tonight."

Aunt Jane was silent.

"And next time we'll go someplace you like."

"I don't see why we can't fly," Aunt Jane said. "It's the driving I don't like but thank you, I'll think about it."

Dolores always said it had been wonderful of Jane to take care of her mother-in-law. "No way!" she had said to Steve after his mother's stroke. "Put her in a nursing home. I can't manage her plus three children, the house, the dog and you. Your mother needs full-time care so don't look at me!"

That was over two years ago – her mother-in-law now dead fourteen months. Dolores doesn't know how many more times she can hold her tongue with Jane. She would like to go on vacation with her husband and children and nobody else. That means I'm selfish, she thought remembering Steve's words last night. I wonder why she doesn't visit Lucas, her own son. He's not even married – has a nice house in Vermont – plenty of room including a studio to paint and money – or so I'm told. One of these days, I'll ask.

"Where did you read about weather-watchers Aunt Jane?" said Steve.

"Didn't. Saw it on television," she said.

"Me too," said Jeff.

"They go right up to the tornado while it's resting. Of course, they have a pretty good idea of what it will do next."

"Good Lord!" said Dolores.

"They call them *the beasts*."

Maggie's red king jumped over two of Jeff's black checkers and trapped his king. "I won!" she said.

"I wasn't even trying," said Jeff. "So it doesn't count."

"The beasts?" said Dolores, a new nightmare forming in her head.

The next morning Aunt Jane was packed and settled in the front seat of the blue Chevy Suburban – next to where Steve would be, her large green suitcase set by the cargo area so he'd see it right off when he came out of the garage. The Targetts watched her from the window of the side door overlooking the driveway. "She can't sit in back – something about it makes her sick," said Steve as if Dolores had asked.

"Poor Bingo, said Dolores."

"He'll be fine at the vet's."

"You should have taken him yesterday."

"I thought Aunt Jane might go home," said Steve.

"Are you sure they're open this early?"

"Someone's got to be there."

Dolores made a face. "If not, Aunt Jane will just have to put up with him. The car holds nine people. God knows there's plenty of room for a little dog!"

Melissa dragged her suitcase down the stairs. "I'm ready!" she said. "Let's go!"

Maggie, Jeff and Bingo were already in the car. Neither Steve nor Dolores had seen them get in. Dolores did a quick sweep of the house. No dirty dishes in the kitchen. They were going to stop for breakfast later on. She straightened the children's beds, plumped the pillows, pulled quilts over them, picked up towels, cleaned two bathroom sinks with the dampest one and threw them all in the laundry basket. She hated coming back to a messy house. Steve plugged in the timers for the lights and locked the doors. It was 6:30 A.M. Almost on schedule. Not a bad beginning.

The Bide-a-way Hospital for Dogs and Cats had an obdurate silence about it. "Sorry, Aunt Jane," Steve said after ringing the bell and knocking hard and long.

"You tried," said Dolores. "Can't be helped." She gave a thumbs-up in the air behind Aunt Jane's head.

"All clear, Bingo" whispered Maggie in his ear, kissing his head.

Aunt Jane didn't believe Steve had tried hard enough: He hadn't gone to the back door; he hadn't shouted and he had waited until the last minute to go to the kennel. Now she'd have to put up with Bingo's bad breath, frequent need to piddle and yips whenever he saw something exciting, which was all the time. He was a horrid little white terrier of some unknown mix her nephew picked up at the animal shelter when he was a pup.

"Tell us about twisters, Aunt Jane," said Steve as if he knew what was on her mind and wanted to change it.

Aunt Jane was pleased. The center of attention was where she felt most comfortable. Her life had been filled with events she liked to tell about. The trouble was nobody usually asked. "When I was young," she began, "your grandma and I and our brothers lived on a small farm in Kansas with our mama and papa – your great-grandparents. Not a whole lot happened that was exciting in those days except a cow got out of the fence or there was a runaway horse. We had one radio and one phone and thought we were pretty lucky because, of course, our parents never had such things when they were children. We didn't even own a car though some relatives did so sometimes we got to go with them to see the show on Saturday night.

"I thought this was going to be about twisters!" said Melissa.

"Melissa!" said Dolores. "Hush up!"

"I'm setting the scene," said Aunt Jane.

"What was the show?" asked Maggie.

"That's what we called the movies – sometimes we said picture show and that was short for moving picture show." I should have been a teacher, thought Aunt Jane. She loved to hear herself explain things.

"Go on," said Steve.

"If you didn't have a car – how did you do your

shopping?" asked Melissa.

"Once a week papa drove mama to the grocers in the horse and buggy. We weren't far from town so we kids walked there when we needed an extra pound of sugar or flour – but we had our own milk, butter, cream, eggs and mama put up tomatoes, beans, peas, peaches, rhubarb, cucumber and watermelon pickles and we kept potatoes, carrots and turnips in the root cellar. Of course we killed our own chickens and pigs so there was always plenty of good food."

"It sounds like a lot of work," said Melissa.

"Well it was but we were used to it. That's all we knew."

"You must be a hundred years old," said Maggie.

"No she's not!" said Dolores. "And that was a rude thing to say. Apologize."

"I'm sorry, Aunt Jane."

"I accept your apology."

"I'm getting hungry," said Melissa.

"There's a good diner off the next exit," said Aunt Jane.

"When were you on this road before?" asked Steve.

"Right after your mother's funeral when Lucas and I drove down to the Keys."

"I didn't know that," said Dolores.

"I probably didn't mention it."

"How is Lucas?" asked Dolores. "You never talk about him."

"Same as always," said Aunt Jane, whatever that meant.

"He seemed fine at the funeral," said Steve.

"He was," said Aunt Jane.

"A diner, you say?" said Steve.

"Sounds good," said Dolores, "but let's sit at the counter so we can get right back on the road. The sky is turning a funny yellow west of us."

"Don't worry." said Steve, "We're headed south and it's farther away than it looks."

"I've seen such skies before," said Aunt Jane.

Steve turned off the highway. It was starting to rain.

"Take a left," said Aunt Jane. "It's not too far – maybe a mile or so on the right."

"Wow, we're heading toward the storm," said Jeff.

"I hear your stomach growling. Gross," said Maggie.

"I hear yours too. Big deal." Jeff punched her arm.

"Mom!"

"There will be no hitting on this trip," said Dolores. "Cut it out now."

Steve drove one, two, three miles. "You sure it was this exit, Aunt Jane?"

"Yes I am. That's too bad. I guess they closed it down. Not enough business maybe."

"No harm done," said Steve looking for a place to turn around.

Just then it occurred to Aunt Jane that the diner she was thinking of was in North Carolina, the next state down. The realization caused her to jump, which made her open pocketbook and everything in it fall on the floor – she'd been searching for her new lipstick – when a double crash of thunder following a series of lightning bolts startled her. She screamed. The dog, with high-pitched barks, leaped from the back seat down her shoulder and onto her lap. She screamed again. The children laughed.

"We've got to stop, Steve," said Dolores. "Poor Aunt Jane."

It was raining harder now. "Okay," said Steve. "I'll just pull into this gas station. Hold on, everyone," he said and braked sharply. As he turned the pickup behind him slammed into his back left fender and the Chevy tipped over to the right, hung there and came back to center.

"Thank God," said Steve as he unbuckled his belt. "You all okay?" he asked as he got out of the car.

"Get this dog off of me," Aunt Jane said. "I think he's peed on my dress and now he's licking my face."

"Jesus," Steve said surveying the damage. The pickup was smashed on the right side – the windshield cracked. Steve's car wasn't as bad but would need body work.

Dolores leaned over Aunt Jane, grabbed Bingo, lifted him up and over Aunt Jane, hugged him, fastened his leash around his neck and opened the door. Sorry, Aunt Jane," she said before flipping her jacket over her head. "My God! The rain is biblical. Here we go, Bingo."

Steve walked around to the driver's side of the pickup. The person behind the steering wheel hadn't moved. Must be in shock Steve thought or didn't want to get wet. It was a young woman – no more than eighteen. He motioned for her to roll her window down a little.

"Too bad about your truck, ma'am. You and I have to exchange information. I'll get the fellow in the gas station to call the police."

"What for?" asked Junie.

"They have to file a report when there's an accident."

"My father's going to kill me."

"No he won't. It was the rain. You couldn't see."

"I saw you and then..."

"Don't say anything. The insurance companies will argue it out. You're okay, right?"

Junie nodded.

"Put your lights on – just sit there and wait."

"Thanks," said Junie.

He heard a siren. "Wow, that was fast. Someone's sure on the ball."

"Oh, God," said Junie.

"Listen," said Steve. "Nobody's hurt, that's the main thing."

There was more lightening then another crash of thunder. The sky was green-purple. Underneath was a dark swirling haze. When did that happen? Steve wondered. Looks bad except at least the rain was letting up.

He walked back to his car and gestured to his aunt to lower the window. "Aunt Jane," he said, "What do think about that sky?"

"Twister sky," she said.

"You sure."

"Yes."

"Hey kids, where's your Mother?"

"Walking the dog," said Melissa. "Daddy, I'm scared."

"We'll be okay – I got to talk to the police and then we need to go somewhere – take cover."

The policeman had his book and pen out. Steve walked toward him.

"Let's make this quick. There are tornado warnings left and right. Give me your license, registration and insurance card."

Steve was ready for him. He signaled Junie to get hers out.

"That's okay. I know Junie – I can write hers down anytime. Right now we all need to get the hell out of here."

"You know her?"

"She's my daughter."

"Oh," said Steve. He saw Dolores and Bingo get back in the car.

The policeman opened the door to the pickup and helped Junie out.

"Hey, I don't have her information!"

"You don't? Okay – follow us."

"Where to?"

"The police station." He waited until Steve was behind him then took off sirens whining.

"Aunt Jane, I'm scared. You know all about twisters. What's going to happen?" asked Melissa.

"Why nothing, honey. When I was a little girl lots of times we went into our storm cellar, pulled the door down above us and waited till the tornado spun itself out. Nothing's going to happen."

"But we don't have a storm cellar," said Maggie.

"It's exciting," said Jeff. Look, the twister's chasing us. We'll beat it, though."

Bingo was shaking. Dolores comforted herself by patting him and kissing the top of his head. "Maybe we should pray," she said.

"Good idea," said Steve.

"Dear Lord," said Aunt Jane. "Dear Lord."

"Help us in our hour of fear," said Maggie.

"How does that child know what to say?" wondered Dolores.

"Protect us from the twister," said Melissa.

"Thank you for letting me see it so close up," said Jeff.

"Thank you for my life, your many blessings," said Aunt Jane.

The police car slowed down. Steve followed it into the parking lot. "Everybody out! Fast!" he shouted. "Leave – all your stuff. Run."

Morning had become night and nearby a huge deep gray shadow rested under a hideous green-purple lid. Steve stood by the door making sure the three children, Dolores and Bingo were inside. "Oh my God!" he shouted. "Aunt Jane!"

Aunt Jane hated losing things; she'd undone her seatbelt and was bent way over looking for her lipstick. 'Must've rolled somewhere during the accident,' she thought. Besides, there was plenty of time. Nothing was going to happen.

Steve watched, paralyzed, his arm holding the police station door open. He could see Aunt Jane, a triumphant smile on her face waving her lipstick at him. Any second now she'd get out of the car and join them.

Just then the beast turned, roared and swallowed the Chevy – then blew away most of a trailer park on its way out of town.

"No!" Steve heard himself holler. "No!"

"I just hope Aunt Jane didn't see it coming," Dolores said later.

Steve put his arm around her. "It was so quick I don't think she felt a thing," he said.

"She promised nothing would happen," Maggie said.

"For once she was wrong," Melissa said.

"She was a good woman," Dolores said.

"We should have flown to Orlando," Steve said. "If we had – she'd still be with us."

"We'd still have our car," Jeff said.

"And," Maggie added, "my cd player."

Dolores began to cry. "We need to call Lucas," she said.

CLUTTER IN THE ATTIC

As soon as I lose ten pounds I'm going to bed with someone other than my husband, although I can't think of anyone I'm attracted to at the moment. There used to be a lot of men who were interested in me – both of the tennis pros at the club, the husbands of my friends, Jamie from the antique store near our ski house, even my youngest son's counselor, seventeen years my junior. I was better looking then – for one thing my stomach wasn't pooching out – I was a size 4, long honey-blonde hair, but I've still a few strong points or so I'm told. I need to focus on those strong points so I won't swallow a bottle of aspirin, like Ellie did a little over a year ago. I know she didn't mean to die but, by the time Hal found her and got her to the hospital, her liver was destroyed.

Ellie was my closest friend. The day before she died, she told me Hal said he wanted a divorce, though he later denied it. But I know she didn't mean to kill herself. I believe she was just trying to get his attention – she called him after she took her last swallow that May morning though he claims he didn't get the message until late that afternoon. I don't know if I believe him. Bing doesn't. We talked about it for a year. He was as upset as I – maybe more so.

The odd thing about Bing having an affair is that he was never much interested in sex, so he wasn't much of a lover. I know because I slept with two other men before Bing and I were married. I guess I was so in love with him I didn't notice his almost nonexistent libido until it was too late. Anything he did made me hot in those days. Now, nothing he does makes me hot, and it doesn't help that when we make love he refers to himself as my "husbie" and other such talk and I have to answer in kind. After all these years it's too embarrassing to tell him to stop. That's not a problem now because, since I found those records and confronted him, we've been sleeping in separate rooms.

If Ellie were still alive, she'd point out revenge is a terrible reason for sleeping with another man. She always made sense, except for when she took all that aspirin, though she'd have freely admitted she did it for the wrong reason. The right reason would have been that she was dying of some horrible disease and didn't want to suffer.

Bing's been with Irene in motels up and down the east coast for God knows how long and I'll bet without benefit of baby talk. It's not as if it happened when he was drunk. I could probably have overlooked that, but this had been going on a long time with a woman I not only knew but liked and admired. I guess I should be grateful it wasn't one of my close friends. Bing promises never to see Irene again even though her gift shop is smack in the middle of the village where we do all our shopping. What do I say when I run into her? There's no etiquette for such an encounter, is there? Someone should write a book on how to behave when things like that happen and murder isn't an option. But on the other hand perhaps, in this case, it is an option. After all, I am the wronged wife. Should I murder Bing, or Irene, or both of them? I wouldn't even know how and I'd be caught immediately and have to spend the rest of my life in prison while our sons, Tommy and Dan, would be scarred for life, as they say. No – sleeping with someone else makes sense. Then I can throw it in Bing's face and we can forgive each other and take a lovely vacation in Barbados before spring.

That means I have to go on a diet immediately. Ten pounds is a lot for someone only a little over five feet. If I don't lose the weight quickly, and thus have my affair this winter, then I suppose I can lose it by summer and we can go to Greece in July. I'm in no rush. That's not quite the whole story. I've been spending more and more time in my room ever since Ellie died. I sleep a lot and can't get anything done. Rosa comes in every day except Sunday to clean, do laundry, fix meals. Even if I lose ten pounds I don't think Bing will ever look at me again the way he used to. If I didn't have so much money I'll bet he'd ask for a divorce, just like Hal did from Ellie, assuming it's true. Well I'm certainly not going to kill myself and leave a third of everything I own to him.

In the beginning we were able to live off his income. Bing was a stockbroker, but after the twins were born in '64 it got pretty tight, so we had to dip into my inheritance – a little of the interest and dividends – and then, later, Bing quit his job because, he said, he hated Wall Street. It bothered him that I hadn't let him invest any of my money which had been set up in a trust fund for safe-keeping long before we met, and I wanted to keep it that way. As it turns out, I was right not to change anything, and he knows it, though managing my assets would have made him an instant golden boy. From then on he taught math at a boys' prep school not far from where we live. It didn't pay well so he also did some tutoring but by the time Tom and Jack were in college, we began using more and more of my money and then he stopped working altogether. That's okay – the principal is still intact even though I've been giving my boys a few thousand a year since they graduated.

My parents were killed in an automobile accident when I was eighteen and, between them, there was a ton of money. Too bad it didn't make Bing and me happy. It might be just fine for a woman to have a lot more money than her husband, as long as he remains ambitious, or at least interested in his work. But that's not how it was with Bing, and I don't know if he was passive all along or if my money made him that way. It never occurred to me until recently, when I analyzed our marriage for the millionth time, that the damn money came between us.

I stay in bed most of the time because I'm tired. The doctor says I'm depressed, but the pills he prescribed aren't helping. Bing says I'm stuck. He tells me I'd feel better if I threw out some of the "damn clutter" in the attic. But nothing makes me happier than to go upstairs and spend an afternoon looking through old photographs, reading old letters, rummaging through piles of sweaters, Bermuda shorts, racks of dresses, and suits, and remembering happy times.

"What's wrong with that?" I ask Bing.

"They keep you in the past," he says. "Don't you get it?"

"No," I tell him – but, even if he's right, I can't cope with the thought of getting rid of anything. If there's something wrong with me it's too late to change – I may not look it, but I'm fifty-eight years old!

I wouldn't mind pushing sixty so much but there's been almost no passion in my life. I was too young to appreciate what little there was and it wasn't nearly enough. The only wildness in my life is in dreams; sometimes, when I'm half asleep, I invent a lover who almost feels real. Ellie and I used to talk about sex –

not in great detail, just enough to know we both missed out on passion in our lives. When I was madly attracted to someone, she was the only one I told. It happened a lot when I was younger, though I never acted on it. Now, because of Bing and Irene, I feel like a fool. I should have slept with Jamie when I had the chance. I was so in love with him. No one would think to look at me now that my mind is mostly on sex. They'd be horrified. I can't help it – especially now that I've been betrayed. I want to say to Bing, "How dare you do that to me?"

It sounds so old-fashioned, but that's exactly the way I feel after all these years of paying the bills and giving parties for his friends. I even paid for his rolls-in-the-damn-hay with Irene, which I still wouldn't know about if I hadn't gone over our credit card statements for the very first time. I saw a TV program about how important it is to check every entry because there might be charges you hadn't made. I still need to go through all those boxes in the attic from years past. What if Bing's been cheating on me even longer? What if he slept with one of my friends? Ellie, for example, although, of course, that's impossible – I'd never believe that. I couldn't be unlucky enough to have been betrayed by both my husband and my best friend. If so – I don't know what I'd do. And what if Ellie killed herself because she was madly in love with Bing and he was cheating on us both with Irene? Maybe Hal knows – he said that at the very end Ellie told him she was sorry. What was she sorry about? I assumed it was for committing suicide by mistake but who knows? Bing and I both thought Hal must be depressed because after she died he stopped playing paddle at the club – Bing and he were often partners – and he wouldn't even come over for dinner though I invited him several times. Of course, that doesn't mean he wouldn't meet me for coffee or lunch. Years ago, he used to flirt with me – like most of my friends' husbands did – and he's by no means bad-looking. What am I thinking? Irene's probably the only other woman Bing's been with. Meanwhile, I'm writing this down as you're supposed to do when you have a mission:

1. Lose ten pounds
2. Fall for someone attractive.
3. Get even with Bing.
4. Go for a vacation in Barbados or Greece.

If there's no bad news in those boxes – that should be that. God help him if there is.

UNDER WRAPS

The best thing is to say nothing. If I tell my husband, Steamboat, he won't believe me, tell me I have some imagination, or am going crazy. He'd be right – I am crazy, crazier than he has any idea of because most of the time, I keep my thoughts to myself. That's not to say I don't observe what is going on around me, that I don't listen very carefully, and that I don't know things, but this is different and, someday, when I have one-too-many drinks, maybe I'll tell Georgia.

It was a calculated risk. When a man keels over at a cocktail party, is taken to the hospital and later dies, it doesn't occur to anyone that he's been poisoned. If he's over fifty and has a history of heart trouble then it's not likely there will even be an autopsy. Even if they cut him open for a look-see, the shock of the poison probably causes a heart seizure, and who would think to check further in Marsbury, the upscale suburb I've lived in for thirty years. I must have figured it right because heart attack was the diagnosis for John Carmody – a man who richly deserved to die and, last week, finally did.

John Carmody's offense took place several years back, but I had to bide my time. I also had to be careful because of our business. Georgia, my partner, and I have been making and serving hors d'oeuvres at local cocktail and dinner parties for more than ten years. Steamboat and I don't need the money, but I like to keep busy. Georgia and I have become very popular because our prices are reasonable, we are neat and tidy, and the food is excellent, even if there's a sameness about our menus. People seem to like the predictability because, if they wanted something really different, we'd oblige. Every year we choose one or two new fillings to offer for our turnovers but it's rare that we are asked for anything beyond the mushroom or spinach.

John was always very flirtatious with me – went so far as to put his hand on my thigh under the table at a dinner party years ago. I pushed it away and didn't think any more about it even though, at the time, I didn't know that it wasn't big girls who caught his fancy. I was looking good in those days, auburn hair, navy-blue eyes, and long legs and so a lot of the men had an eye for me. I wasn't interested in an affair – I'd had my share of men in the six years between marriages – although sometimes I acted like I found guys who came on to me attractive so they wouldn't take offense and try to hurt me.

Men don't like it if you reject them – so if anyone came right out and said something provocative, I'd act like I didn't get it. That's probably one of the reasons I have a reputation for being a bit thick. It's much safer that way. Georgia, whose daughter was molested by John when she was five, had a reputation for being sharp, but where did it get her? She's divorced now and never has put her life together. Her husband, Chas, didn't believe their daughter's story, and I'm not saying that's the reason they eventually divorced, but it played a part. John and Chas played a lot of golf at one another's clubs. You better believe Chas wasn't about to give up going to Stony Hills, the most prestigious golf club in the county, for the sake of a little girl with a vivid and disgusting imagination.

You're wondering why Georgia didn't report him. It was different in those days. John Carmody was an important, wealthy man, the father of four, president of a large corporation and, later, the mayor of our town, and he would have denied it categorically. Who would have believed poor little Emily? Georgia's family – there were two other children – would have had to leave town or, at the least, move from where they lived – right across the street from him and his family. It was unheard of for a child to accuse an adult of doing something so terrible, so forbidden, and Georgia couldn't swear to it. She wasn't there in the Carmody's basement when John asked Emily to come down with him – to choose what kind of ice cream he should bring upstairs for the neighborhood kids. Georgia found out later that Emily had gone with him before and what he did the other times wasn't as flagrant. He also made Emily promise she wouldn't tell her mother. For certain, if she'd asked her mother for permission to go with him, Georgia would have said, "Of course!"

Emily and her brothers were often over there, mostly outside – playing with the Carmody kids and others in the corner lot next door. You can be sure that Georgia would have been labeled hysterical if she told the police John put his hand down Emily's shorts and underpants while placing her hand on the thing poking out from his madras trousers. She was quietly hysterical, just knowing what had happened and having to pretend things were okay. What could she do? Not invite his family to parties any longer? Yes. Avoid them? Yes. Wish him evil? Of course. Hope his wife would somehow find out about it so he wouldn't do it to anyone else? Yes, but that never happened. Georgia would have seen a change in Leila's behavior if it had. She didn't tell me a word about it until much later and, by then, I was married to Steamboat. He's my third husband. The second one died. I'd like to say he died of the heart attack that's on the death certificate but then you're way ahead of me, aren't you?

If there is ever an article about me in the newspaper the headline will say something like Suburban Killer or Marsbury Murderess, as if I were a raving maniac who slept with a knife under my pillow, or poison in the garage, and sent people to their eternal rewards because I was in a bad mood. No, not at all. I'm a nice, ordinary person – still better looking than average, well educated at a prestigious junior college and, under ordinary circumstances, I wouldn't hurt a damn fly. It amazes me as much as it would my dear Steamboat if he knew I could accomplish such a thing cool as you please, without a minute's regret, and my heart not skipping a beat, or my hands clammy. It's a strange talent to recognize you have when you're nearly forty-five years old, and I suppose you could say I wish someone did know because I am, God forgive me, actually proud of it. The point is that some people get away with murder in this world and that it's not always so terrible – as in my case, for example – because when a grown man does horrible, unforgivable, things to a child – it's worse than murder.

I married at nineteen after discovering I was pregnant. Olivia's father was the same age and, even then, I couldn't understand why I had been so dumb as to have sex with him except that I was drunk. It was my first time, wouldn't you know. Didn't even enjoy it. We never lived together but in those days you just didn't have a child out of wedlock. I met Lou, my next husband, when Olivia was three.

I was modeling in the city and taking an occasional photography class whenever I had the money. He was dating a friend of mine but when he saw me that was it and he loved the fact that I had a little girl. He wanted to marry me then and there, wanted me to stop working. He had inherited property and other assets, sold insurance and annuities and made a bundle, so money wasn't a worry anymore. We moved to Marsbury – a half-hour train ride from the city. It had a great school system – still does. He was fifteen years older, had a bit of a heart condition, but I was attracted anyhow. He was just so nice to us both – that was it. The sex was pretty good too.

As a special treat, when Olivia was a little older, Lou sometimes took her to his workshop – a little room attached to the garage with its own heater where he made things out of wood – not big projects, but wonderful tiny animals, planes, cars and houses. Olivia, who was then about six years old, was particularly fond of painting them. I can't tell you how happy this made me. I grew up with a cold, remote sort of father, a naval officer, who disliked me or acted as if he did. Having Lou be such a good dad to my daughter was an extraordinary thing. I had no idea such men existed. He was always home on the weekends, loved to work in the garden, loved puttering around the house, loved my cooking, loved us. I should have known something was wrong. I should have known if something seems too good to be true – then, of course, it is.

I see now that I always had a secretive, plotting side to my nature – I often photographed my neighbors from the porch when they were carrying in their groceries or working in the yard. I took my small Leica everywhere I went; it used Tri-X film that didn't require a flash, but did require a steady hand. Sometimes I would hide in my car near the school so

I could photograph children on their way home. I didn't have my own darkroom – after all there was nothing unusual or x-rated about the pictures. Why did I do this? I found it interesting to catch people off guard without anything fake on their faces or in their poses – people as they really were, which, I told myself, helped me to see myself as I really am. I wouldn't keep many of the pictures, just the best ones, and there were more and more that were good. In September, 1979 I decided to take a picture of Lou and Olivia while they were at work together. I thought I would have it blown up and framed to give each of them for Christmas. Before they went up to the "shop" I told them I was going food shopping – then I left the house, got in the car, and drove off. Actually, I did a couple of quick errands before I returned, parked the car at the school, a block and a half away, and walked to the back of our house through a lane abutting an empty lot. The window was still open that morning; there was no screen, which was a problem in the warmer weather – flies, hornets, bees, but we never got around to doing anything about it. I thought I would have a clear shot of Lou and Olivia together.

I was right.

Before I realized what the camera was seeing, I had already taken the picture. I had moved over from the side of the house, quickly framed them in the viewfinder, and held down the button. It was perfect. They hadn't looked up. They hadn't noticed me. Until I screamed they had no idea I was there.

When Georgia described what John Carmody did to Emily I couldn't help but tell her what had happened that September morning long ago. She was horrified, said it was even worse than what John did to Emily because Olivia thought of Lou as her father. She was right. It brought the scene and what followed back to me. I obsessed about it for weeks until I decided to take matters of life and death into my own hands on behalf of my good friend.

I don't remember running to the workroom and grabbing Olivia but I do remember opening the door to the house and locking it. My purse and camera were on the ground outside the garage where I dropped them. Once inside I kept thinking it was important to get them before Lou did but, as it turned out, he didn't come out of the room until lunchtime an hour later and I guess he never saw the camera in my hands at the window. I suppose he zipped up his pants and kept on creating his toys. When he came to the house he couldn't open the door, so he came around to the front. I'd locked that, too. He went back up to the workshop and got some tools so he could cut one side of our porch screen and then once inside – because the lock on the porch door was broken – he just walked in. He came into the kitchen where I was holding Olivia on my lap and kissing her over and over. I couldn't speak – I couldn't feel – and there was the man I loved two feet away. But I knew at that moment I could never love him again. How do you move from love to hate? It doesn't happen right away, or it didn't for me, and that was what was as horrible as what he'd been doing.

"Mary-Ellen," Lou said.

By then, Olivia and I were on the stairs. We said nothing. Lou continued,

"It seems I have a problem " He was standing at the bottom of the steps, sort of swaying and holding onto the banister. Was he drunk?

"A problem? That's it?" I was shocked.

"Go on upstairs, honey." I said to Olivia.

I turned to face him.

"In less than a month she won't even remember," he said.

I wanted to scream at him, tell him he was a monster, tell him I hated him, tell him to get out and never come back and God knows I would have if Olivia weren't in the house – if I weren't afraid of frightening and hurting her even more than she must have been already, but I was silent, my brain drowning in this terrible new knowledge. In the photograph, when I had the strength to develop it, I knew I would see a face I'd never seen before – another Lou.

I didn't know what to say to Olivia. We read stories all afternoon. By dinner time I decided to pretend everything would work out somehow. I still didn't know what I would do. I wrote a note to Lou and left it on top of the mail in the front hall. It read, "Please move all your things into the guest room. I don't want to see you or talk to you. You'll have to eat out."

First grade was not going to start for a week. I decided to take Olivia to my mother's for a few days while I sorted everything out. We flew down to Virginia Beach where Olivia and I often went in the summer for weeks at a time – where we'd been most of July – and twice a day took her across the avenue to the beach, dragging an umbrella, chairs, books, drinks, snacks, suntan lotion and hats.

My mother kept asking me, "What's the matter?" I just said, "Lou and I need some time to ourselves."

The second afternoon lying side by side on our towels Olivia turned toward me. "Mom," she said.

"Yes, honey."

"Remember that day you were mad at daddy?"

"Of course."

"He said it was all right if I did what he asked me to do. He said you wouldn't mind but that I shouldn't tell you. It was a secret," she said.

"I see."

"It was just a game."

"Was that the first time you played the game with Lou," I asked.

"No," she said.

"Do you remember how many times before?"

"Not really," a few, I guess."

"How did it make you feel?"

"Sort of sick to my stomach," she said.

"When we get back home we'll find someone nice for you to talk to about it."

"Why?'

"Just to be sure you don't ever get sick to your stomach again."

"Was it a bad thing?"

"A very bad thing."

"Are you mad at me?"

"You? Good heavens, honey, not a bit."

Olivia relaxed. Funny I hadn't noticed how tense she'd been. It never occurred to me she thought I was upset with her. Some mother I was. I was so focused on Lou, my desire to find a way to punish him – I didn't pick up on Olivia's feelings.

It was on the plane returning to La Guardia that I decided to ask Lou for a divorce. The house and some other assets would be mine and he'd pay me alimony. He'd put aside a fund that would be locked away earning interest for Olivia's education. I would continue to own the insurance policy of a million on his life. He'd never ask to see her or me again. I felt sure he would say yes, that he'll be glad not to be reported to the police, his family, my family, our friends.

I was wrong. Lou laughed when I outlined my plan.

"No divorce," he said. "I love you and Olivia. I made a mistake that's all and no one will believe you if you tell them about it. No one!"

He didn't even feel real remorse. He didn't show a shred of guilt.

"How can we have a normal marriage after what happened?' I asked him. "How can I ever trust you again?"

"You'll get over it," he said.

I can't think of anything that would be the right thing for him to have said, but that was definitely not it. If he'd said he was sorry it wouldn't have helped – but you'd think he'd at least have said it. All this time I was thinking I have proof of what happened on a roll of film he knew nothing about. But did I want to go through a contested divorce, did I want the world to remember the sight of Olivia holding Lou's penis? Not on your life.

That's when I decided to make Lou a mushroom omelet for dinner the next night. Had this been in my mind the whole time? Maybe – because the idea came to me so easily: Buy some mushrooms for me to eat that are the same color as the ones in the woods near our house – the ones Lou often pointed out to Olivia and me as poisonous. Pick the deadly mushrooms – clean, slice them and put in a Ziploc bag in the back of the refrigerator. Ditto my mushrooms, except put them in the front. Make his favorite salad of arugula, endive, scallions, red pepper and dill – and his favorite dessert, apple clafouti. Delicious. It really was. Every bite. I should mention that a crushed

Sumatriptan pill was another ingredient in the omelet – I take them to reduce blood flow when I have a migraine.

Only eighteen hours later in the hospital when Lou, according to the nurse, could hear but no longer speak – I told him his omelet had contained the deadly amanita bisporigera. Before you knew it he stopped breathing – so maybe he had a heart attack after all. Anyway, that's what the death certificate said.

As for John Carmody, Georgia was serving him a drink when he became dizzy and collapsed – Jack Daniels and water all over the carpet; I was still in the kitchen. She kept her head and called 911. We hardly spoke going home. I couldn't think of what to say and Georgia seemed in shock but when I dropped her off she poked her head back through the door and said, "If he dies, my prayers will be answered. Should I feel guilty?"

"Of course not," I said.

I'd like to have told her I was the guilty one but she'd have thought I was crazy, crazier than I ever really was. She'd never in this world believe I could pull off a thing like that. No one would. The best thing is to say nothing.

Earlier, I got John Carmody to follow me into the kitchen where I popped a warm mushroom/ Sumatriptan turnover in his mouth.

"I've been saving this special one just for you, John."

He was intrigued. "Why?" he asked.

"Because you deserve it," I said.

No, I hadn't planned to say that. Sometimes you just get lucky.